The Howling In Griffin Forest

By Penelope Dyan

Bellissima Publishing, LLC
Jamul, California
www.bellissimapublishing.com

Copyright © 2022 by Penny D. Weigand

All rights reserved. No part of this book may be reproduced or transmitted in any form or by any means, electronic or mechanical, including any photocopying, or recording, or by any information or storage retrieval system, without permission from the publisher and author.

ISBN 978-1-61477-617-8

First Edition

"All creatures great and small have their special place on this earth of ours!"

PENELOPE DYAN

About The Author & The Book

Penelope Dyan became a teacher, an award winning published writer, a vocalist, and a mother and an attorney, all while following her dreams! And her happy life proves one hundred percent that dreams really do come true!

It was the lifelong experiences of the author, Penelope Dyan, and her great desire to do good in this world, along with her love for nature's creatures and her deep concern for others, that led to the creation of this book, "The Howling In Griffin Forest", her fourth book about Griffin Farm, filled with a host of familiar characters you are certain to enjoy and a message you will not soon forget.

Say 'hello' once again to Janie and her family and (of course) say 'hello' to Mrs. Carter (as well) and find out why Janie's mother spoon-feeds a dog named Runty, and how Runty saves the day!

Most of all, never forget to follow your dreams, just like Janie is following her dreams. And never, ever forget that love and courage exist in all creatures great and small, and that even from a spoon-fed dog we can learn a lesson about courage, and caring, and love.

The Howling In Griffin Forest

By Penelope Dyan

The Howling In Griffin Forest

CHAPTER ONE

THE NIGHT BEFORE BREAKFAST

"Did you hear all that howling coming from out back in the forest last night?" Janie asked, as she sat down at the breakfast table.

"Sure did," Janie's father told her, in a mumble. "It was probably because it was the last supermoon of the year."

"What's a supermoon?" Janie asked.

"It's a scientific phenomenon that happens when the moon appears particularly large in the sky, because it is coincidentally on its closest approach to the earth, when there also happens to be a full moon, which is also called a 'new moon'."

"Oh," Janie said, not really understanding exactly what her father was saying.

"It was really something," Janie's mother interjected. "I barely slept a wink!"

"Well, it didn't exactly help when our dogs joined in with all of the howling," Janie's father added, yawning.

"I think they were just singing," Janie told her parents. "It was a full moon, after all, and a supermoon to boot!"

"And who are *they*?" Janie's father asked her.

"You know," Janie told her father.

"No. I don't know. You said they were singing. So, who was singing? Witches? Ghosts? Things that go bump in the night? You must be precise!" he teased.

Janie laughed.

"Well, we don't have any wolves here in Virginia, so what caused all the howling?" Janie's father continued with the tease.

"The coyotes!" Janie exclaimed. And then she asked, "But whatever happened to the wolves? Where, oh where, is the big bad wolf?"

"Well, red wolves and grey wolves used to thrive in Virginia, but now they only live here in national parks," Janie's father told her.

"What happened to them?" Janie asked.

"I imagine they were hunted into extinction," Janie's mother interjected, as she came from the kitchen and placed a piping hot plate of Belgian waffles on the already set table and headed back to the kitchen for the butter and maple syrup.

"How sad," Janie said, as she helped herself to one of the Belgian waffles, and her father helped himself to two!

The Howling In Griffin Forest

"I love these things," he said, as Janie's mother placed the butter and maple syrup on the table.

"Enjoy!" Janie's mother told them.

And then, between mouthfuls of waffle, Janie asked, "Are coyotes dangerous? I mean, can they attack and hurt you?"

"Not usually," Janie's mother told her, as she sat down at her place on the table and prepared her breakfast plate. "But, as with all things, especially wild animals, you should never go looking for trouble. And they will attack cats, rodents, and small dogs and the like."

"Well, we certainly don't have any small dogs!" Janie's father scoffed. "But we should look after the outdoor cats and the chickens and such, I guess."

"I think the outdoor cats know better than to mess with them," Janie's mother said. "And we do put the chickens and what not in at night."

"And our Andalusian herd dogs do keep everything safe," Janie's father added, as Janie listened ever so intently.

"Does that mean we have our own little balance of nature here?" Janie asked.

"Well, sort of," Janie's father told her. "Just don't go messing around with those things!"

"By things, do you mean coyotes?" Jane asked, teasing her father now for his lack of preciseness.

The Howling In Griffin Forest

"Precisely!" Janie's father told her.

And then, the three of them laughed; and Janie's mother suddenly popped up from the table and hurried into the kitchen!

"I forgot the freshly squeezed orange juice!" she said.

"You work way too hard!" Janie's father yelled after her. "But I do love freshly squeezed orange juice," he whispered in a quick side comment to Janie.

"Me too!" Janie told her father.

And when Janie's mother returned, they all settled down to finish a very fine breakfast! And (of course) Janie's parents had to have their cups of morning coffee!

And so, they did! And so, the day began!

CHAPTER TWO
THERE ONCE WAS A PUPPY!

There was once a very special puppy born on Griffin Farm, a puppy Janie's mother helped introduce into the world.

"I'm a dog midwife!" Janie's mother exclaimed, as she helped Abigail, the mother Andalusian dog give birth to the last of her six pups, as Janie watched the entire process out in the barn where Cheery Day resided.

"Something's wrong!" Janie excitedly exclaimed, as it was obvious the puppy was not breathing.

Janie's mother took the pup and placed it in the towel she had brought with her to the barn.

"Don't worry, Janie!" Janie's mother told her. "I'm not going to give up on this one."

Janie's mother vigorously rubbed the puppy in the towel in which she had carefully placed the pup.

The Howling In Griffin Forest

"He's still not breathing!" Janie said excitedly, somewhat terrorized they might lose the tiny, newborn pup. "And he's so much smaller than the rest!"

"Good things always come in small packages," Janie's father said, as he entered the barn unannounced.

Janie's mother had an idea.

"I'm going to try some mouth-to-mouth resuscitation!" she announced.

"Eew! Really?" Janie asked. "That sounds so gross!"

Janie's mother said nothing, as she began the procedure and as Janie's father watched.

And then, what seemed like a miracle to both Janie and Janie's father, the puppy gasped for air.

"It's a miracle!" Janie exclaimed. "It's a real life miracle!" she exclaimed again.

"It sure is!" Janie's father excitedly shouted.

"Well," Janie's mother said, "I figured if your grandmother could sew up a goat that had been attacked by her neighbor's dog, this was the least I could do!"

And then, she set the puppy next to the pup's mother so the two could bond and so that the pup could begin suckling its mother's milk, which *did* finally (at last) transpire, as the three of them watched.

In the back of the barn Cheery Day whinnied, as if she knew what was happening at the front of the barn; and the barn cats scampered about the barn, keeping a safe distance from the new mother.

However, unfortunately, this was not the end of the story in regard to this particular pup!

CHAPTER THREE
WHAT HAPPENED NEXT

Now, while Janie's mother was able to save the pup, while the other puppies were weaning and being put on dry food, it was obvious there was something wrong with the special puppy Janie's mother had saved. He couldn't eat. And when he tried to eat, he became very sick. (And, of course, his mother was no longer interested in nursing him once she had weaned the other pups.)

Since he was born last, and because he was the smallest of the puppies, Janie's mother named him 'Runty'. And truth be told . . . Janie and her mother, and even her father, were all quite fond of Runty.

"What are we going to do?" Janie asked her mother, as they watched the other pups eating heartily, while Runty sat on the outside of the feeding area. "Why won't he eat?" Janie asked.

"Maybe he knows it will make him sick,' Janie's mother replied.

"But he has to eat! He just has to eat, or he will die!" Janie said, as tears streamed down her cheeks.

Janie's mother went to Janie's side and hugged her.

"It will be all right," she told Janie. "I'm going to take him to the vet."

"You aren't going to put him down are you?" Janie asked. "You aren't going to put him down like some people put down lame horses, are you?"

"Of course not! We all love Runty! I'm going to find out what is wrong with him. And that's all! And then we'll figure out how to help him with the help of the vet," Janie's mother explained, as Janie wiped the tears from her cheeks, leaving a couple of somewhat dirty streaks under her eyes, because her hands were dirty from her chores.

"Okay," Janie said. "But do you think we might try bottle feeding him like we did with those two abandoned kittens we found last year?"

"Now, that's an idea!" Janie's mother told her. "And it's worth a try! And I just happen to have a couple of cans left of that milk replacement under the kitchen sink cupboard!"

"What about the bottles?" Janie asked

"I still have those," Janie's mother told her. "But I think he's kind of big for those. I'll have your dad pick up another larger bottle from the feed store on his way home from work," she added, as she quickly speed dialed Janie's father and gave him the directive.

The Howling In Griffin Forest

"Anything for you and the kidlet!" Janie's dad told Janie's mother.

"And for Runty!" Janie's mother replied.

"And that goes without saying!" Janie's father said, somewhat kiddingly.

And after hearing the news, Janie smiled, her face still somewhat streaked with dirt.

"You really need to wash that face of yours," her mother told her.

And after that, Janie's mother called the vet and made an appointment for the next afternoon.

"And don't forget to bring the dog!" the veterinarian's receptionist joked.

"Janie's mother laughed.

"Oh, I won't," she said. "That little guy is very important to us!"

The Howling In Griffin Forest

CHAPTER FOUR
TO THE VET AND OUT THE DOOR

That next afternoon, while Janie was having her training lesson with her trainer, Mrs. Carter, Janie's mother scurried out the door, hopped into the family truck with Runty, and headed into town for the veterinarian appointment.

"It appears this pup has megaesophagus," the veterinarian told Janie's mother after carefully examining Runty on the examination table, and after listening to the issues the pup was having, as presented to him by Janie's mother.

"Whatever is that?" Janie's mother asked.

"It's basically an inflammation of the esophagus, that makes it difficult for a puppy to eat. And it's usually discovered after weaning the puppy, which coincides exactly with what you told me," the veterinarian explained.

"Did I cause it when I resuscitated him when he was born?" Janie's mother asked, as she worriedly patted little Runty on his head.

"Megaesophagus can be either congenital or acquired, the veterinarian explained. "But when a newborn pup isn't breathing there really is no choice as to what to do, when your instincts take over, but to render aid in the form of resuscitation," the veterinarian patiently explained. "And, in fact, there is often no known actual cause. They are simply born with the condition. And megaesophagus is usually not even diagnosed until the puppy is weaned, as in the case here with little Runty."

"So, this wasn't my fault?" Janie's mother asked.

"Now, I can't say for certain, but my best guess is that this little guy was born with this particular genetic defect," the veterinarian further explained.

"Is there anything I can do?" Janie's mother asked. "My daughter will be heartbroken if we lose this little guy."

"Yes. There is always something a dog owner can do; but it will take a bit of work, time and determination on your part," the veterinarian explained. "And I can tell you exactly what to do!"

"Okay!" Janie's mother told the veterinarian. "Just tell me what needs to be done."

"He can't have dry dog food, only canned and human foods, but they need to be heavy foods. He'll have to eat sitting up, and you'll have to spoon feed him or drop the food into his mouth. And some dogs sit in a special chair to facilitate this."

"I can do that!" Janie's mother told the veterinarian.

"Well, then I believe this pup can live a relatively long and prosperous life; and we will see how this goes for him," the veterinarian said. And then he added, "However, there is one more thing . . ."

"What's that?" Janie's mother asked.

"You may have to burp him," the veterinarian told her. "In fact, you probably should."

"Oh, I can do that, too!" Janie's mother replied with a smile.

"And . . ." the veterinarian added, "if he starts aspirating or coughing a lot, call me right away. Runty may need an antibiotic or other further treatment."

"I can do that as well!" Janie's mother emphatically replied.

And so, it was done. And before the family knew it, little Runty was seventy-five pounds and growing! However, all of the in-between parts of this story are better left to another time and another place and another story! However, needless to say, whenever Runty got hungry, Janie's mother was at his apparent beck and call.

CHAPTER FIVE
STAYIN' ALIVE

Now that keeping Runty alive was number one on Janie's mother's list of things to do, she stopped by the grocery store on the way home for two cases of canned dog food, for which she negotiated a ten percent discount on the final price.

As she placed dinner on the table that night, to the usual oohs and aahs, she endeavored to explain what the veterinarian had told her to Janie's father, Janie and Mrs. Carter (who continued to refuse monetary compensation for working with Janie and Cheery day, preferring to instead partake of the evening meal with the family).

"Well, it is indeed good that you found out what was ailing the poor little pup," Mrs. Carter said, as Runty began to wail from where he was sitting on a nearby staircase.

Meanwhile, Pinkerton, the dog, whined and scratched at the kitchen back door.

The Howling In Griffin Forest

"Well, it looks like our zoo is moving into the house," Janie's father said jokingly.

No one laughed.

"I guess I'd better take care of Runty," Janie's mother said, just as Runty stopped his wailing, relieving her for the moment of the task of spoon feeding him.

"Saved by the bell!" Janie's father exclaimed. "Or should I say saved by the cessation of the wail?"

Janie shook her head, as her mother squirmed a bit nervously in her seat.

"I'm sure I can get little Runty on a schedule," Janie's mother said. "Please be patient with me," she added. "I just can't help but to think I may have been the cause of his condition."

"But why ever would you think that?" Janie asked. "You saved Runty's life!"

"That's what the vet said," Janie's mother replied. "But I just worry I hurt him somehow."

"I'm sure you did nothing of the sort," Mrs. Carter told Janie's mother in the most serious tone. "You made a choice to bring life to him when he wasn't breathing. You gave that pup the gift of life!"

"And that makes you his mother!" Janie's dad interjected with a smile.

"And if I'm his mother, are you his father?" Janie's mother asked with a raise of her eyebrows.

The Howling In Griffin Forest

And then everyone laughed.

And when the laughing subsided, they all returned to the meal.

"The stroganoff is delicious!" Mrs. Carter said. "I must have your recipe!"

And as to that, Janie's mother agreed, as the bowl of peas and the homemade cranberry sauce were in turn passed around the table.

And later, for dessert, they had raspberries atop vanilla bean ice-cream. And the adults had their coffee, as little Runty slept.

After dinner, the table was cleared; and once the dishes were done, with Mrs. Carter insisting on helping with the task (for which Janie's mother thanked her profusely) Mrs. Carter hopped into her old, 2002 Ford F150 white pickup truck, and she headed right back into the city.

Janie and her mother waved goodbye to Mrs. Carter, as Janie's father sat in the living room watching the evening news on their widescreen TV.

And later, Janie's mother spoon fed and burped Runty, as the veterinarian had told her she must, and as she would continue to do (from now on) many times over, and over again! After all, Runty was now her baby; and she had (for all intents and purposes) taken over the role as his mother.

And this was because Janie's mother had a kind and loving heart.

CHAPTER SIX

Pickup Sticks

"Have you ever played a game called 'Pickup Sticks'? Mrs. Carter asked Janie, as Janie began removing the jumps from the bed of Mrs. Carter's old 2002 Ford white pickup truck, as Cheery Day stood tied to the practice ring's rail, and as Pinkerton, the dog, stood patiently next to Mrs. Carter, as Mrs. Carter stood next to her old pickup truck, leaning on her cane.

"No," Janie replied with furrowed brow. "Does it have to do anything with riding?"

"Well, not really, and sort of," Mrs. Carter told Janie.

Janie raised her eyebrows.

"I don't understand," she told Mrs. Carter, as she waited for an explanation, and as she removed the last jump from the pickup truck, and as she set it on the ground next to the other jumps, just outside the gate of the practice ring.

The Howling In Griffin Forest

"Well, you drop these thin, differently colored sticks that are about eight to ten inches long into a loose pile onto a tabletop or onto the floor where the players are sitting. (And, of course, there are two or more players, although the game can be played alone.) Each player, in turn, tries to remove a stick from the pile without disturbing any of the other sticks. The object of the game is to pick up the most sticks, and the player that picks up the most sticks without disturbing any of the other sticks wins the game!"

"I've never heard of that game," Janie told Mrs. Carter. "It sounds like fun."

"Well, it is fun! But the purpose of the game is more than that. It's a game of both physical and mental skill, because you have to coordinate hand and eye movement, as you think in a strategic manner," Mrs. Carter explained. "And that's why it's like riding. When you ride, you must carefully consider everything around you; and you must think in a strategic manner, as you coordinate hand and eye movement, as well as the movement of your own body and the body of the horse under your direction."

"Wow!" Janie said. "That sounds like some game!"

"It is! I played it as a child, and it took me all the way to performing as a trick rider in the rodeo!" Mrs. Carter told Janie, as she leaned upon her cane.

And after that, Janie set out the jumps; and as she and Cheery Day made each jump under the tutelage of Mrs. Carter, Janie thought

The Howling In Griffin Forest

about what Mrs. Carter had said. And once practice had ended, Mrs. Carter presented Janie with a gift! It was a brand-new box of pickup sticks!

"I'll teach you how to play the game later," Mrs. Carter told Janie.

And then, as Mrs. Carter drove her pickup truck back to the farmhouse, and as Janie sat atop Cheery Day, with Pinkerton, the dog, at their side and with the box of Pickup Sticks held in Janie's free hand, Janie followed closely behind, and she couldn't help but to smile.

And meanwhile, Mrs. Carter wondered what gastronomic feast Janie's mother had prepared for dinner.

You see, Mrs. Carter was now a member of the family; and she loved this family dearly.

CHAPTER SEVEN

MADE IN HEAVEN

Janie's mother decided to fix her famous secret recipe fried chicken that night for dinner. And Janie and her father couldn't have been more excited about that!

The secret to Janie's mother's famous secret recipe fried chicken was simple. First, you season the chicken, then you dip the chicken in flour, making sure it's completely covered, and then you fry it; and after you fry it, you bake the chicken at 350 degrees in the oven until fully cooked.

And even though Janie loved her mother's fried chicken, according to Janie (and she was quick to tell you this) it seemed like a lot of trouble to go to just to cook a chicken! But everyone, including Janie, had to admit as they sat down to eat the chicken, mashed potatoes and gravy, homemade cranberry sauce, coleslaw and green beans . . . that not a fried chicken on earth could top Janie's mother's secret recipe fried chicken, even if it was (in the end) mostly baked! And besides, it was the baking of the chicken in the oven (after the frying) that gave the juices from the chicken that made that delicious gravy!

"This is a regular feast!" Mrs. Carter exclaimed, as she began to eat. And then she asked, "How is the bee business going?"

Janie's mother sighed.

"Well, it's not going as well as I would have liked it to go, Mrs. Carter," she said. "With having to feed Runty several times a day now, it has become difficult to get down to Rose's (the bee lady's place) as often as I would like, or for as long as I would like."

"I'm sure she understands," Janie's father interjected. "We are all country folk, albeit our entrance into the farm scene is not as well established as some folks out here."

"Yes. I'm sure she understands," Mrs. Carter said between continued mouthfuls of chicken. "And by the way," she added, "this chicken is absolutely delicious!"

Janie's mother smiled.

"Well, I did manage to get down to Rose's place for a few hours today; and I may be bringing home a surprise soon," she said.

"A surprise?" Janie asked. "I just love surprises!" she added. "So, what's the surprise?"

The Howling In Griffin Forest

"If I told you it wouldn't be very much of a surprise," Janie's mother told Janie, teasingly. "And besides, I still have to clear it with your father."

"Please don't tell me you're bringing home the bee lady's entire honeybee business," Janie's father quipped.

"Oh, no! It's nothing like that," Janie's mother told him. "So, don't you worry one single bit about that!"

"Well, then . . . I am quite puzzled," Janie's father told her.

"I'll give you a hint," Janie's mother replied. "And the hint is that we don't have one."

"Well, at least it's only one!" Janie's father laughed.

And then, nothing more was said on the subject; and when the meal was over, Janie's mother served a dessert of orange sponge cake topped with whipped cream, along with coffee for the adults and a large glass of milk for Janie.

And later, after Mrs. Carter drove off in her old 2002 white Ford F150 pickup truck, Janie went out to the barns to finish her chores, all the time wondering about the surprise that was to come.

CHAPTER EIGHT
"I Simply Can't Wait!'

The next morning at breakfast, Janie begged her mother to tell her more about the illusive surprise!

"Please tell me! Please! Please! Please!" she begged.

Janie's mother smiled, as she poured Janie's father a second cup of coffee, after he'd finished eating his blueberry waffles with maple syrup.

"You cook a fine breakfast!" he said, as Janie continued to implore her mother to tell her what the surprise was.

"I know something you don't know," Janie's father told Janie in a sing-song tone of voice.

"Well," Janie said, as she sopped up the last bit of maple syrup on her plate with her last bite of blueberry waffle, "that hardly seems fair!"

Janie's father laughed and repeated again in his sing-song tone of voice, "I know something you don't know!"

The Howling In Griffin Forest

"That's not fair! That's just not fair!" Janie protested. "Why does Dad know what the surprise is, and I don't?"

"Well," Janie's mother began, "remember when I said your father had to approve the surprise?"

"Yeah . . ." Janie mumbled.

"Well," Janie's mother continued, "that's why he knows what the surprise is, and you don't. You see, since he had to approve the surprise, it becomes our surprise from the two of us to you!"

Janie shook her head.

"Well, then . . . when will I find out what the surprise is?" Janie asked the two of them.

"Let's just say it will be sooner rather than later," Janie's father teased.

"And what does that mean?" Janie asked.

"If we tell you what that means, that will spoil part of the surprise," Janie's father half-heartedly explained.

"What your father means to say," Janie's mother then added, "is showing you the surprise is part of the surprise."

"So, that means you won't tell me what the surprise is, or when I will find out what the surprise is?"

Not exactly," Janie's father told her.

Janie sighed.

"So, what exactly are you saying, exactly?" Janie asked.

The Howling In Griffin Forest

"I am saying that everything will be known to you sooner rather than later," Janie's father said with a grin, to which Janie just shrugged her shoulders, knowing that when her father began playing word games with her, there was no value in trying to figure out what he was saying.

And so, Janie helped her mother clean the table and do the dishes, and she headed out to complete her daily chores.

Janie decided she would just have to wait. After all, Janie's father did say it would be sooner, rather than later! So, the waiting couldn't possibly be that long. At least that was what Janie hoped. You see, Janie was never very good at waiting for anything. Like her grandmother in California, everything had to happen right away; and waiting for tomorrow was almost never an option, especially when it came to surprises. Waiting for Christmas Day was bad enough! And this wasn't even Christmastime!

CHAPTER NINE
"Please Don't Whine!'

After Janie came in from doing her evening chores, she begged her mother and her father once again to please tell her what the surprise was.

"I just can't wait!" Janie pleaded. "Please, please, pretty please, tell me what the surprise is, or I swear I won't be able to sleep tonight."

"Please don't whine," Janie's mother told her. "All good things happen in their own good time."

Then, Janie's dad took off his glasses and stopped watching the wide screen TV, turning down its volume, as her mother went into the kitchen to fetch a pitcher of ice-cold lemonade and three carefully stacked plastic drinking glasses, all of which she managed to carry back to the living room, without the use of a tray.

Janie's father said nothing and waited for Janie's mother to return to the room.

The Howling In Griffin Forest

Once the three drinking glasses were placed on coasters, and the pitcher of lemonade was set on an old magazine, saved for this purpose, Janie's dad asked, "Well, should we tell her, mother? We do want the kidlet to sleep tonight!"

Janie's mother smiled rather wryly.

"Well, why not?" she replied

"I can't think of a reason for not telling her that outweighs the issue of the kidlet not sleeping tonight," Janie's father said, as Janie's mother sat down on the couch, and as Janie stood before her father who sat comfortably sipping his lemonade as he remained sitting in his overstuffed armchair, Janie's mother having previously both placed and filled his glass as it sat on the end table next to his chair.

Janie's mother decided to play along with the subterfuge for just a bit longer.

"I don't know if we really should tell her right now," Janie's mother said. "The excitement of actually knowing what the surprise is just might keep her up all night anyway."

"Please! Please!" Janie pleaded with her mother.

"You know what would taste really good with this lemonade?" Janie's father asked.

"I sure do!" Janie's mother said, as she headed into the kitchen and returned with the cookie jar and a handful of napkins.

The Howling In Griffin Forest

"I hope that's filled with those chocolate chip cookies you were baking last night," Janie's father said, as Janie sighed impatiently.

"It sure is!" Janie's mother exclaimed. And then she added, "And by the way, did you happen to notice the shape of this cookie jar, Janie?"

"Well, it looks like the head of a cow," Janie said. "But why are you asking me that?" Janie asked her mother.

"Think about it," Janie's father told her. "What animal do we *not* have in our Griffin Farm zoo?"

Janie looked back and forth at her parents, with a wide-eyed, questioning look.

"Do you mean we are going to get a cow?" she asked.

"Yes! That's exactly what we mean!" Janie's mother exclaimed.

"Oh my!" Janie said, astonished at the thought of it.

"Why are you saying, 'Oh my'?" Janie's mother asked.

"You were right," Janie told her, as Janie lowered her gaze. "I'm so excited I won't be able to sleep, for sure!"

Janie's mother sighed, and then the coyotes began to howl, as they did every night; and Janie's mother (after finishing her cookies and her glass of lemonade) went into the kitchen where Runty was waiting to be spoon-fed his dinner.

And Janie was simply full of questions!

CHAPTER TEN

"Please Tell Me AGAIN!'

Janie simply could not believe they were getting a cow; and as she was laying in her bed that night, she uncharacteristically asked her mother to 'tuck her in' (as her mother walked by her bedroom door) much to her mother's great surprise.

"Is something wrong?" Janie's mother asked, as she entered Janie's bedroom.

"I just can't believe we're getting an actual cow!" Janie told her mother.

"Why? Don't you like cows? We have just everything else, when it comes to animals, so why not a cow?" Janie's mother asked Janie.

"I love cows!" Janie told her mother. "I've always secretly wanted a cow, but I was afraid to ask for one. So, will you please just tell me again that we're actually getting a cow, so I can believe that it's true?"

The Howling In Griffin Forest

Janie's mother smiled and patted Janie's head as she sat down on Janie's bed next to Janie.

As Janie's dad was walking past Janie's bedroom door he heard what Janie was saying; and he couldn't help himself, but to add a little something to the conversation.

"Well, don't have a cow over it!" he joked, but Janie didn't think it was funny.

"Are we really, truly getting a real live cow?" Janie asked.

Janie's father, standing in the doorway, smiled.

"We are really, truly getting a real live cow," Janie's mother told Janie.

Janie's eyes widened, right along with her smile.

"Is that your cartoon face?" Janie's father asked.

"It's my happy face!" Janie exclaimed. "I'm just so excited and happy!"

Do you want to know more?" Janie's mother asked her. "Or maybe, you want the rest to be a surprise?" she asked.

"Oh, tell me more!" Janie told her mother.

"Like what?" Janie's mother asked.

"Well, is she an old cow or a young cow?"

"She's a young cow, Janie," Janie's mother told her.

"Well, then," Janie went on, "has she ever had a calf?"

"No. She has never had a calf." Janie's mother answered.

"Does she have a name?" Janie asked.

The Howling In Griffin Forest

"I don't know, but I don't think so! And I do believe we can name her anything we like," Janie's mother told Janie.

"What kind of cow is she?" Janie asked.

"She's a jersey cow," Janie's mother said.

"Well, then, I have one more question."

"Ask, then," Janie's father said from the doorway.

"Can we breed her, and can I milk her? And can I join 4H at school? And when will she come home here to Griffin Farm?"

"I do believe that was four questions," Janie's father scoffed, still standing in the doorway. "And the answers are . . ."

"The answers to the first two questions are 'maybe', the answer to the third question is, 'we shall see' (because you do have a lot on your plate). And the answer to the fourth question is I will bring her home tomorrow afternoon and you can visit with her after your training lesson with Mrs. Carter!" Janie's mother interjected.

And at that point, Janie faked a frown and when she finally managed to fall asleep, she dreamed of beautiful cows with wings flying through the air! And (of course) Pinkerton, the Dog, slept soundly on the floor beside Janie's bed, always and forever ready to jump into defense mode.

CHAPTER ELEVEN
THE SURPRISE ARRIVES!

Janie was a bit distracted at her training session that day. Luckily, Cheery Day knew exactly what to do as they went through the paces, and as Pinkerton, the dog sat at Mrs. Carter's feet patiently watching.

Janie and Cheery Day went around and around in the ring, going through various phases of equitation. And Janie knew she was distracted, so she was glad they weren't working the jumps. After all, she didn't fancy falling off Cheery Day during a jump.

Mrs. Carter sensed Janie's distraction; and at the end of the session, she asked, "Is something bothering you, my child?"

Janie smiled at the thought that Mrs. Carter would refer to her as a child, because she knew Mrs. Carter only thought of what she was saying as an endearment.

"Besides," Janie thought, "It's better than being called a kidlet!"

The Howling In Griffin Forest

Mrs. Carter waited for Janie to answer, as Janie got down from atop Cheery Day and patted Pinkerton, the dog, on his head.

"We're getting a cow today!" Janie exclaimed. "Or rather, Mom is bringing one home after she visits Rose, the bee lady."

"Oh my, that is exciting!" Mrs. Carter exclaimed.

"Maybe we can use a real cow to rope now!" Janie suddenly blurted out. "I'm still doing western showing, right?"

"You can do whatever kind of showing you like," Mrs. Carter told her. "That's why we train in both fields."

"So, do you think I can practice roping and herding on a real live cow?"

I don't see why not," Mrs. Carter told Janie. "But as with all things, we must wait and see,"

"Wait and see what?" Janie asked, as Cheery Day veered her head in the direction of the automatic waterer next to where they were standing.

"Well, this is a new addition to the farm; and we don't want to upset the poor dear," Mrs. Carter said. "We must assess her temperament and decide whether subjecting her to training will cause her undue stress."

Janie thought for a moment.

"I guess you're right," she told Mrs. Carter. "But I'm very interested in joining 4H, and this could be my opportunity!"

Mrs. Carter smiled.

The Howling In Griffin Forest

"Do you even know what 4H is all about?" Mrs. Carter asked.

"Not exactly," Janie told her. "But I do know it has to do with showing animals at the county fair. And that sounds like a lot of fun."

"It's also quite a lot of work," Mrs. Carter told Janie. "I used to be in 4H when I was your age, so I know that for a fact."

"Oh, I don't mind hard work, Mrs. Carter. I really don't."

Mrs. Carter smiled.

"If I decide to do something with 4H, do you think you could help me?" Janie timidly asked. "I mean, I wouldn't ask you to do anything big. I just might need some advice."

"Of course, I'll help you!" Mrs. Carter told Janie. "It will be both my honor and my pleasure!"

And now it was Janie's turn to smile!

"The next thing she'll be wanting to learn is trick rodeo horse stunts," Mrs. Carter thought to herself, as she shook her head in silence, quite pleased at Janie's new interest, and not worrying a bit that Janie would overextend herself.

In Mrs. Carter's mind, Janie could do and accomplish anything she set her heart and mind to do.

And then, Janie spotted her mother pulling the family truck and horse trailer next to the barn where Cheery Day's stall was.

"She's here! She's here!" Janie screamed excitedly.

"Well, then . . . I do believe introductions are in order!" Mrs. Carter told Janie, As Janie hopped onto Cheery Day (who was now finished drinking at the automatic waterer) and she and Cheery day, and Pinkerton, the dog (of course) headed toward the barn where Janie's mother was busily unloading the newest member of their family, a beautiful, young, two-year-old Jersey heifer.

And Mrs. Carter followed behind in her old, white 2002 Ford F150 Pickup truck.

CHAPTER TWELVE
THE NAMING OF THE COW!

    Janie brought Cheery Day to a full gallop, which was quite unlike her, because she usually liked to cherish and enjoy every single moment atop her precious mount. However, today was different! Today, Janie was about to come face to face with her very own cow! (At least that was how Janie saw it.)

    Janie practically jumped off Cheery Day; and together, ever so slowly (out of pure caution) she and Pinkerton, the dog, and Cheery Day entered the barn, Janie holding onto the leads of Cherry Day's harness and bit.

    And there she was! She was in the very first stall! (The cow, that is.) And Janie's mother was standing right there in front of the stall waiting to welcome the small troop into the barn.

"Isn't she just beautiful?" Janie's mother asked, as Mrs. Carter's old, white, 2002 Ford F150 pickup truck could be heard rolling up to the outside of the barn.

"She sure is!" Janie exclaimed, with her eyes sparkling with excitement.

"Do you think I would spook her if I came closer to her?" Janie timidly asked her mother.

"Of course not!" Mrs. Carter's voiced boomed out as she entered the barn. "You've got yourself a regular beauty there!" she told Jamie's mother. "And I see she's a well-bred jersey!" she added.

"Does she have a name?" Janie asked.

"I dunno!" Janie's father's voice boomed out, as he entered the barn, just behind Mrs. Carter. "Does she have a name, mother?" he asked.

Janie's mother grimaced.

"I am *not* your mother!" Janie's mother told him.

Janie's father laughed.

"Well . . . does she, or doesn't she, have a name?" he asked, repeating Janie's question.

Mrs. Carter stood by quietly.

"Can she be my cow?" Janie asked. "And if she's my cow, can I name her if she doesn't have a name already? I mean, if she already has a name we should call her by that name, or she might get confused or something."

"Well, I don't know about her being *your* cow," Janie's mother told Janie. "I think she should be sort of autonomous."

"What does that mean?" Janie asked, as her father pulled out his cell phone and quickly googled the word, 'autonomous'.

"Well, defining the word very loosely," Janie's father began, "it means having the freedom to act independently."

What do you mean by 'defining the word very loosely'," Janie asked her father.

"Well, usually the word is used to describe countries or school boards and things like that," Janie's father said, as he gave Janie's mother a certain look with which she was all too familiar.

"I think what your mother is trying to say," Mrs. Carter then interjected, "is that this fine jersey should choose for herself to whom she belongs."

"Yes! Exactly!" Janie's mother told her. "Just like all of us, she should have the freedom to independently choose in matters such as these."

"You mean like Pinkerton and Cheery Day chose me?" Janie asked.

"Precisely," Janie's mother told her. "But that said, since this cow has no name, and because she needs a name, you may (indeed) name her!"

Janie smiled.

The Howling In Griffin Forest

And then, without hesitation, Janie picked up a nearby shovel, held it up right next to her (shovel side up) as if it was a queen's scepter, and proclaimed, "Given the power vested in me, I now dub thee and forever grant thee the following name! Now and forevermore you shall be named, 'Faith'!" Janie told the cow.

And everyone agreed that the name 'Faith' was a very fine name granted to the cow before them in the stall. And no one asked why Janie had chosen that particular name. It simply was what it was, as all things happened to be and were meant to be.

And Faith stood quietly in her new stall in her new home, as Pinkerton looked on, and as Cheery Day whinnied.

"Why, I think Cheery Day is welcoming Faith into the family!" Mrs. Carter exclaimed.

And then, everyone laughed.

And it was a very good day, indeed!

CHAPTER THIRTEEN
AND LATER CAME DINNER!

Later, as Janie, Mrs. Carter and Janie's father waited for Janie's mother to bring out the dinner, the talk was all about Faith, the jersey cow. And Janie was simply full of questions, and she was most interested in finding out the answer to one single particular question!

"How did jersey cows get their name?" Janie asked.

And (of course) out came Janie's father's mobile phone where he quickly googled the question.

"It says here that the Jersey is a British breed of small dairy cattle that came from Jersey in the British Channel Islands," Janie's father told Janie, always happy that his kidlet was full of questions; because that meant she was learning new things.

Janie laughed.

"That's silly," Janie told her father. "I mean, why would a cow be named after a place in the British Isles?"

(Janie's father didn't even *try* to look *that* up on his mobile phone.)

"Well, kidlet," he told Janie, laughing. "Some things just are what they are for no rhyme or reason!"

"Then, I guess it is what it is!" Janie exclaimed.

"Yes, I do believe it is so!" Janie's father teased, as Janie's mother set a pot roast, that was on a large platter with all the fixings, in the center of the previously set dinner table.

"I don't believe I want to eat that," Janie said, somewhat decisively.

"But why not?" Mrs. Carter asked. "It looks and smells delicious," she added as Janie's mother returned to the kitchen to fetch the gravy and homemade cranberry sauce.

"It's a cow!" Janie exclaimed. "And someone killed it!"

"Well, it's not exactly a whole cow," Janie's father told Janie, as Janie's mother returned with the gravy and homemade cranberry sauce.

"But you have eaten cow before this and never complained," Janie's mother said, as she took her place at the table, and as Janie's father stood up to slice the pot roast into serving size pieces.

"But that was before," Janie said.

"Before what?" Janie's mother asked.

"Well," Janie began, "that was before I looked into Faith's big brown eyes."

The Howling In Griffin Forest

And then, Janie's mother understood. You see, she couldn't eat pork for the longest time, because back in California where she grew up, she once had a pet pig!

"Well then," Janie's mother told her, "you just eat the potatoes and carrots and cranberries, and don't worry about a thing."

Janie smiled; and for the first time, when presented with a pot roast at the table, Janie's father decided not to call this dinner, 'roast beast'! After all, the term 'beast' sounded too much like something that could be construed as being akin to a cow, and he would rather not upset his dinner.

And that night, as Janie slept, with Pinkerton, the dog, laying beside her bed, she dreamed of an entire island full of Jersey cows romping amongst vast pastures of green.

And outside, in Griffin Forest, the coyotes howled.

CHAPTER FOURTEEN
BUT HOW CAN WE AFFORD IT?

The next morning at breakfast, reality was beginning to settle in for Janie's father, as he perused the lasts prices on the feed invoices, set before him as he ate his scrambled eggs and toast.

"Well, mother," he said, as he looked up from the pile of bills and invoices, "with prices going up everywhere as they are, I'm beginning to wonder how we will be able to afford to feed all of these animals."

Janie's eyes grew wide.

"We aren't going to get rid of any of them, are we?" Janie asked, as she set down her fork full of scrambled eggs onto her plate. "I don't think I could stand that!"

Janie's mother took a sip of her orange juice.

"No. We're not going to get rid of any of the animals," Janie's mother said, decisively.

"We'll just stop feeding you!" Janie's father joked, as the tears swelled up in Janie's eyes.

Janie wasn't laughing.

"I have an answer for everything!" Janie's mother said.

"For everything?" Janie's father asked.

"Well, for almost everything," Janie's mother replied.

"What does that mean?" Janie asked.

"Well, first of all, I did a little research on sustainable feed alternatives and contacted a few people; and early today I got a reply from a local brewery."

"I don't get it," Janie told her mother. "What are sustainable feed alternatives?"

"Well, in this case, it happens to be grain used for something else," Janie's mother began. "And in this particular case, what I was able to find out, after a lot of research and many, many calls, was that breweries use grain in the making of beer, and when the beer has brewed they have to do something with all of that spent grain."

"And?" Janie asked.

"And if your dad agrees, we can partner with a local brewery to pick up the used grain and use that to supplement the feed of some of our grain eating animals! And what is in excess of what we need, we can give away to the other local farmers!"

"Well, I agree!" Janie's father quickly exclaimed. "I agree!" he repeated.

The Howling In Griffin Forest

"And the good news is that the people who are picking up what we don't use here (or what we can't use here) are giving us donations for gas! So, we get the feed for basically nothing! Of course, we may have to supplement the feed; but I think it will save us quite a lot on our basic budget!"

Janie's dad smiled.

"How soon can we get started?" he asked.

"It's Saturday. So, is today too soon?" Janie's mother asked.

Janie's father smiled.

"It's perfect!" he exclaimed. "And the only cost to us will be in our labor, which we have to do anyway, even when we pay for feed!"

"And we have plenty of storage bins and space in our barns!" Janie's mother added. "And while not all of the animals can eat it, it will supplement our feed bills for those who can't."

Janie smiled.

"So, when do we leave?" Janie asked.

"You're staying here, Janie. We leave (your father and I) when Mrs. Carter comes to give you your training lessons," Janie's mother told her. "And she said she would stay with you until we get back."

"But what about dinner?" Janie's father asked.

"I'm making crockpot stew with the pot roast leftovers, and I'll bake some very fine baking soda biscuits! I already have the biscuit dough in the refrigerator, and the stew in the crockpot; and everything will be delicious!"

"But I don't eat beef, remember?" Janie protested.

Janie's mother smiled.

"In that case, you will have a fried egg sandwich with mayonnaise, and a generous portion of the salad I will be serving!" she told Janie.

And then, all was right with the world; and Janie set about doing her chores (as well as the morning dishes) as her mother announced (as she hurried out the front door) that she was off to help Rose, the bee lady, with the hives, and that she would be bringing home a jar of honey for the dinner's biscuits.

CHAPTER FIFTEEN
HOW NOW PRETTY COW?

Janie decided to spend the rest of the day in the barn with Faith, at least until Mrs. Carter arrived for Janie's training session with Cheery Day. And, of course, Pinkerton the dog was right there in the barn with Janie.

Janie decided not to go inside Faith's pen, fearing that if she got too close to the cow, it just might poop on her or something; and so, she sat outside Faith's pen door inside the barn and had a long heart to heart talk with her.

What was said that day after chores to that jersey cow was of little importance, because (after all) a jersey cow can't return a response in a conversation other than to say, "Moo"; and Janie simply did not speak the language of cows! Suffice it to say that the two of them and Pinkerton, the dog, were simply getting to know one another. And (of course) because Cheery Day knew Janie was in the barn, she let out an occasional whinny!

The Howling In Griffin Forest

After a while, Janie's tummy began to grumble; and before Janie knew it, her mother, now back from the bee lady's house, was calling Janie back to the farmhouse for lunch.

"Well, since you no longer eat meat, how about a bagel with cream cheese and a nice fruit cocktail and whipped cream salad?" Janie's mother asked, as Janie entered the back door that led into the kitchen.

Janie's father came down from upstairs wondering what was for lunch and was very pleased to hear they were having bagels and cream cheese and the fruit cocktail and whipped cream salad.

"I don't think you could ever go wrong with whipped cream!" he exclaimed as he sat down at the kitchen table that was already set before him.

Janie's father reached for a warm bagel, as Janie's mother brought in the fruit cocktail and whipped cream salad and set it on the table.

"Ambrosia!" Janie's father exclaimed. "I do love Ambrosia salad!"

Janie looked at her father quizzically, as she took a bite of the bagel she had just opened and smothered with cream cheese.

"Ambrosia is the salad the gods ate on Mount Olympus," Janie's father told her.

"But doesn't that salad have to have coconut and miniature marshmallows and maraschino cherries and orange slices in it and

The Howling In Griffin Forest

stuff like that?" Janie's mother asked Janie's father, as she set the bowl of fruit cocktail with whipped cream on the table.

"There are many, many versions of ambrosia salad," Janie's father replied. "And I am heretofore proclaiming this salad as one of them! It is truly the salad of the gods!"

Janie giggled.

"He's only saying that because he likes whipped cream," Janie's mother said, as she sat down at the table.

And Janie nodded her head in agreement, as she continued to chomp down on her bagel with cream cheese.

And then, Janie's mother reminded the two of them that when Mrs. Carter arrived that day for Janie's lesson, that she and Janie's father would be heading out to pick up the spent grain.

So far, it had been a very busy day for Janie's mother. However, what needed to be done had to be done, and today was the day for doing it!

And not long after that, the phone rang. And Mrs. Carter, according to plan, announced she was on the way to the farm.

Janie didn't understand.

"Why is she coming so early?" Janie asked.

"Because she's helping us out!" Janie's mother told her. "I don't want you alone out here with all that howling going on in the forest. Who knows what could happen?"

"Janie grimaced.

"I'm a big girl now," she said. "And besides, the howling only comes at night."

"You're not *that* big!" Janie's mother protested. "And besides, Mrs. Carter just wants to be a part of things. She's like family!"

Janie shook her head in agreement.

"Yeah, I guess she is part of the family now," Janie said.

"She certainly is!" Janie's father agreed.

"But I'm still a big girl!" Janie proffered.

"No. You're our kidlet!" Janie's father said, as he took a big scoop of his now renamed ambrosia salad from the bowl on the table, and quickly stuffed a spoonful of it in his mouth.

Janie laughed.

"You're so funny," she said.

"Keep laughing," her father told her. "Laughter is the very best medicine of all!"

"Well, I can't very well laugh and eat at the same time," Janie told her father.

"So, eat!" her father replied.

And then, nothing more on the subject was said.

CHAPTER SIXTEEN
THE DAY GOES ON

Janie wondered if the spent grain her parents went to get would smell like beer and if the animals who *could* eat it as a feed supplement would actually like it. She surmised it was one of those wait and see things; and since her mother researched everything on the internet, she decided that in the end everything would more than likely be okay. Otherwise, she supposed they might have some very inebriated (or sick) animals on their hands.

Mrs. Carter arrived a little early (as expected) and so Janie rode Cheery Day out to the practice ring with (of course) the ever-faithful Pinkerton, the dog, running alongside them.

"I brought the jumps," Mrs. Carter said, as Janie arrived at the ring with her small entourage.

Janie knew what *that* meant, and so she quickly hopped off Cheery Day and began unloading the jumps.

The Howling In Griffin Forest

"And I have plenty of chilled orange Gatorade in the cooler inside the cab of the truck Mrs. Carter added.

As Janie set out the jumps, Cheery Day became somewhat uneasy and began to paw at the ground and shake her head as her nostrils flared and her long mane flew in the wind.

"What is going on with Cheery Day?" Mrs. Carter asked, as Janie returned to her horse to mount her and begin the training session.

"I don't know," Janie told her. "But she is acting a bit strange today. Do you think it's because of Faith, our new jersey cow?"

"I doubt that," Mrs. Carter told Janie, as she handed Janie a bottle of chilled orange Gatorade she'd removed from the cooler earlier, as Janie set the jumps out in the ring.

"You need to hydrate," she told Janie. "It's still rather warm, and summer has not yet ended.

Janie took the chilled bottle of orange Gatorade from Mrs. Carter, opened it, and took a good, long drink.

"Thank you," she said, between swallows. "This really hits the spot!"

"That's what it's supposed to do," Mrs. Carter told her.

As Cheery Day continued to erratically paw the ground, Janie said, "Maybe we shouldn't train today. Maybe something's wrong with Cheery Day. She never acts like this."

"I think she may be trying to just tell us something," Mrs. Carter said, as she stood leaning on her cane, looking all around her.

The Howling In Griffin Forest

Janie climbed up the rails of the practice ring with the bottle of orange Gatorade still in her right hand.

And then they saw it! They saw what was upsetting Cheery Day!

"Oh, my goodness!" Janie exclaimed. "Do you see what I see?"

"Yes," Mrs. Carter replied. "I do believe I do."

And then, Cheery Day whinnied; and Pinkerton, the dog, began to bark, although he remained where he was.

"It's a pack of coyotes!" Janie exclaimed.

"And then, the coyotes disappeared back into the forest just as quickly as they had been discovered; and Pinkerton, the dog, stopped barking, and Cheery day returned to her normal state of being, and the lesson resumed.

After all, with the problem for all intents and purposes now gone, it was the only logical thing to do!

And so, Janie hopped aboard Cheery Day, and they jumped the jumps. And Pinkerton, the dog, stood faithfully next to Mrs. Carter watching it all.

CHAPTER SEVENTEEN
AT THE END OF PRACTICE

Janie's parents returned, a short while after practice had ended, with a flatbed (hauled by their truck, of course) filled with barrels of spent grain, a share of which they unloaded and placed in the barns. Quickly thereafter, several of their neighbors, from up and down the road, appeared with their pickup trucks to take *their* share of the spent grain; and each of them gratefully chipped in some money to cover the related costs of both Janie's parents' time and the money Janie's parents spent on gas, as they had promised they would.

"That's very kind of you," Janie's mother told each one of them in turn. "Now, just remember to use the spent grain quickly before it spoils. Because you don't want to feed spoiled spent grain to your animals, or they could get sick and die. If you haven't used your share within three days, you can use it for compost," Janie's mother went on to explain. "And please do your research on this just as I have done."

The Howling In Griffin Forest

Each of the neighbors agreed, in turn, as they loaded their individual pickup trucks with their share of the barrels of spent grain.

"And don't forget to return the barrels," Janie's mother told them. "Because we'll be exchanging those empty barrels for full ones on our next grain run."

Everyone agreed.

And later, after they all had left, Janie ran to her mother and father and asked, "Is this worth all of this trouble?"

And hearing the posed question, Janie's father said, "With the price of grain being so high now, it certainly is!"

"And besides that," Janie's mother added, "we are doing one more good thing for the environment!'

And then, as Janie's father took the truck and flatbed with the few now remaining barrels of spent grain back to the barns, Janie and her mother walked back to the farmhouse front door where Mrs. Carter was waiting for them, leaning on her cane.

As they entered the farmhouse door, Mrs. Carter knowingly said to Janie's mother, "You are doing a very good thing!"

And as to that, Janie's mother simply replied, "Waste not, want not!"

And then, the three of them went inside the farmhouse where Janie's mother went into the kitchen to ready the (now early) evening meal, with the unasked-for help of Janie and Mrs. Carter who had followed her into the kitchen.

"You work very hard," Mrs. Carter said, as she removed the dinner plates from the cupboard to set the table, and as Janie grabbed the silverware from the kitchen drawer next to the sink, both ready to set the table.

"A little hard work never hurt anyone," Janie's mother said with a smile.

But truth be told, Janie's mother was indeed very tired after such a long day, and she was most grateful for the help in readying today's now early evening meal; and so, she told Mrs. Carter exactly how grateful she was, indeed. And Mrs. Carter smiled.

"And now I know where Janie gets her hard work ethic from," Mrs. Carter said.

And hearing that, Janie's mother smiled again; because it felt very good to simply be appreciated.

CHAPTER EIGHTEEN
AT DINNER

Janie's mother quickly set out the beef stew she had created from the previous night's dinner, complemented with homemade baking powder biscuits, butter and honey, and said, "I suppose I'll soon be churning butter from the cream I skim off the milk from Faith."

Janie was astounded at hearing this.

"Do you mean our brand-new Faith is going to calve?" Janie asked.

"That's exactly what I mean!" Janie's mother exclaimed. "And it's all very exciting!" she added.

"I don't know where you get all your energy," Mrs. Carter told her.

"Said by the woman who ran with the rodeo circuit as a trick rider?" Janie's mother affectionately interjected.

The Howling In Griffin Forest

"Maybe I can raise the calf and show it at the county fair as my 4H project," Janie added, as her mother left the room and went into the kitchen, quickly returning with a bowl of tossed salad with vinaigrette dressing, and a fried egg sandwich with mayonnaise for Janie.

"We mustn't let Janie live on just buttered biscuits and honey," Janie's mother said, as she set the bowl of tossed salad on the table and the fried egg sandwich with mayonnaise on Janie's empty plate.

"Now," Janie's father began, "just how long do you intend to keep up this 'no eating meat' thing?" he asked.

"I don't know," Janie said, as she picked up the uncut sandwich and took a bite. "This is quite delicious!" she added.

And then, Mrs. Carter announced she had an announcement!

"So, what's the big announcement?" Janie's father asked her.

"The big announcement is there is another hunter jumper show coming up this weekend, and I think we should enter Janie and Cheery Day," Mrs. Carter replied.

"And?" Janie's father asked, intuitively feeling there was something more that needed to be said, due to how the subject was broached.

"And I want to enter Janie and Cheery Day at a higher level of competition," Mrs. Carter added. "I think I should enter them at level six."

The Howling In Griffin Forest

"But that's the highest level!" Janie's mother protested. "Don't you think it's a bit soon for that?"

"Not at all," Mrs. Carter told Janie's mother. "Not at all," she repeated.

Janie's mother looked over at Janie's father and shook her head as if looking for some kind of support.

"Don't look at me," Janie's father told her. "Have you seen the two of them out in that ring? It's just like poetry in motion! It's just like poetry in motion!" he repeated.

"I'm ready!" Janie piped in excitedly. "Let's do it!" she exclaimed with a smile.

"All right! All right!" Janie's mother then said. "I'm obviously out voted here. I guess I have no other choice but to agree!"

And then they all settled down to their dinner; and because it was a long, tough day, bowls of vanilla ice cream, topped with strawberries and whipped cream were served as dessert, along with the apologies of Janie's mother, all because she felt she should have baked a pie or a cake or cooked up something fancy.

"This entire meal was simply delicious!" Mrs. Carter told Janie's mother. "Please do not apologize for anything," she added.

And then, as the sun went down, the howling in Griffin Forest began once again.

CHAPTER NINETEEN
FEEDING RUNTY

Besides everything else that Janie's mother had to do, she also had to continue to spoon feed Runty.

"How long are you going to have to keep doing that?" Janie's father asked Janie's mother, as Janie bounded out the door to do her chores that next morning after breakfast.

"I think forever," Janie's mother said. "But I suppose a miracle could occur."

"Is it worth it?" Janie's father asked.

"A life is always worth saving," Janie's mother replied.

Janie's father sighed.

"I suppose so," he said. "But it's an awful lot of trouble with everything else you have to do around here."

"I love this puppy," Janie's mother said, as a matter of fact. "And I will bet you dollars to donuts that someday this puppy will pay us back in a big way."

The Howling In Griffin Forest

"I hope you're right," Janie's dad said, as he poured himself a third cup of coffee and headed to the living room, dressed in his slippers, pajamas and robe, to catch the Sunday morning news on their wide screen TV. "That puppy already weighs nearly seventy-five pounds!"

Janie's mother continued to spoon feed Runty, undaunted by the comments of Janie's father. She just had a feeling about this dog that she couldn't explain.

And has she continued to feed Runty, even *she* wondered why she was drawn to this hapless pup. She only knew she loved him, and she just had this feeling about him that she couldn't explain.

And after a while, and just as she was finished feeding Runty, Janie bounded through the back kitchen door.

"I'm finished with my chores!" Janie exclaimed. "Do we have time to go to church today?"

"I think you'd better shower first," her mother told her. "You smell a bit ripe."

Oh, that's because I slipped and fell in a pile of cow manure," Janie giggled.

"Janie's mother shook her head in dismay.

"Well, I guess those sorts of mishaps are merely a part of farm life," she told Janie. And then she added, "Go on upstairs and take off those dirty clothes and put them down the clothes chute and take a shower!"

The Howling In Griffin Forest

Janie scurried upstairs, took off her clothes and threw them down the upstairs clothes chute that led straight down to the laundry room; and when Janie's mother finished spoon feeding Runty, she dutifully put those clothes into the washing machine with the appropriate amount of laundry detergent, and she began the washing machine's cycle, setting it to the proper cleaning level.

"My work is never done," she sighed.

And then, she told Janie's father to get ready for church (and of course, she got ready for church as well) and before they knew it, they were in their double cabbed truck and on their way to church.

And then, after church they headed back home. And because today was Sunday, Mrs. Carter would not be giving Janie a riding lesson. However, she *was* invited to come for Sunday dinner.

And before they knew it, the day had flown past; and there was a knock on the farmhouse door. And (of course) it was Mrs. Carter.

Janie ran to greet her.

"You're just in time for Sunday dinner!" Janie exclaimed, as she opened the front door.

"And I can't wait!" Mrs. Carter, in turn, exclaimed. "Your mother is a very, very fine cook!"

And as to that supposition, Janie wholeheartedly agreed!

CHAPTER TWENTY
THE NEXT DAY

    The next day was a very busy day for all concerned. Janie's father hurried off to work in the city. And Janie's mother set about doing all of her usual things, which (of course) included spoon feeding Runty his morning breakfast, sauntering down to Rose's (the bee lady's house) to assist her with the honey business (as they were now unofficial partners of sorts) scurrying back home to mop the floors, fix lunch for her and Janie, do the laundry, spoon feed Runty again, and other assorted tasks; and Janie had to do all her chores as well, feeding and mucking the stalls, and catching up on her summer reading.

    You see, Janie figured if she read enough during the summer, at least her book reports would be covered for the coming school year when she wouldn't have so much free time. And besides, training with Mrs. Carter and Cheery Day was a year around thing, whereas in summer she had a break of sorts, at least from going to school.

The Howling In Griffin Forest

And so, when Janie's chores were done, she just curled up in the hay in the barn with Cheery day and Faith, Pinkerton (the dog) at her side, and took the book she carried in her pocket and simply read. And it all seemed quite logical to do things that way.

For lunch, Janie's mother fixed grilled cheese sandwiches and tomato soup for the two of them, honoring Janie's recent commitment not to eat meat. And of course, there was a pitcher of freshly squeezed and sweetened lemonade.

As Janie and her mother sat at the table, Janie's mother asked, "What were you doing for so long in the barn?"

"I was reading a book and spending some time with Faith and Cheery Day," Janie told her.

"What's the name of the book you're reading?" Janie's mother asked. "When I was your age I liked Laura Ingalls Wilder books."

"I'm reading 'Little Women'," Janie said. "The girl named Jo in the story reminds me of Grandma."

"But why is that?" Janie's mother asked.

"Well, the girl in the story is a writer, just like Grandma is. So, I think it's kind of cool. And it's about sisters. And that's cool too."

Janie's mother smiled.

"The main thing about reading is to enjoy it," Janie's mother told Janie, to which Janie agreed.

"I do love to read," Janie told her.

The Howling In Griffin Forest

"So do I," Janie's mother confessed. "I just don't seem to have the time for reading anymore."

"Maybe you should make some time for it," Janie told her mother. "You do so much . . . and you deserve to take some time for yourself."

"But how? And when?" Janie's mother asked, as if talking to herself and trying to figure out the answer to that question herself.

"Well, why don't you just make some time for it, some you time?" Janie suggested more than asked. "Let me help you some more. I could help you with dishes and the laundry!" Janie emphatically suggested.

Janie's mother smiled.

"Well," she said, "you do need some time just to be a kid . . ."

"Oh, I have plenty of time for that!" Janie told her mother.

Then Janie's mother thought some more.

And then she told Janie, "How about when you finish a book, you give it to me to read? And then, I'll read it when your dad watches TV and all the chores are done."

"That sounds great!" Janie exclaimed. "And then, we can talk all about the books when we're both done reading them! I would love that!"

"So would I," Janie's mother told her. "And maybe we can even go to the bookstore together and buy some books and build our very own forever library!"

The Howling In Griffin Forest

"I would love that! I just love books!"

"You're just like your grandmother in so many ways," Janie's mother told Janie. "Not only does she write books, she has books in bookcases that reach floor to ceiling!"

"In California?" Janie asked.

"Yes, back in California," Janie's mother told her.

"I sure would love to see that!" Janie said excitedly.

"Well, you *have* seen it. You just don't remember. But someday we will visit your grandmother and grandfather, and you can see it all again," Janie's mother said. "But we are quite busy with the farm right now, so I'm afraid it won't be anytime soon."

And then, shortly thereafter, the postman arrived at the street mailbox with a package of books. They were from Janie's Grandmother, and Janie couldn't wait to read them. You see, the books were all about Griffin Farm (at least they were about how Janie's grandmother imagined Griffin Farm) and Janie couldn't have been more pleased!

But the books were merely fantasy, and the truth was much more exciting!

CHAPTER TWENTY-ONE
THAT AFTERNOON

Shortly thereafter, that afternoon, Mrs. Carter drove up to the farmhouse and back to the practice ring where Janie, Cheery Day and Pinkerton, the dog, were waiting.

As usual, Janie unpacked the jumps, removing them from the bed of Mrs. Carter's old, white, 2002 Ford F150 pickup truck and set the jumps out in the ring, as Mrs. Carter looked on, leaning on her cane, and as Cheery Day patiently, waited tied to the practice ring railing, and as Pinkerton, the dog, decided to do something different, following Janie around the ring as Janie set up the jumps.

"Now, you do know you can't come out here while Cheery Day and I are jumping," Janie told Pinkerton, the dog, as she set up the last of the jumps and the two of them returned to where Mrs. Carter stood leaning on her cane, with a chilled orange Gatorade in hand for Janie.

"Never forget to hydrate!" Mrs. Carter said, as she handed the Gatorade to her young protégé.

Pinkerton, the dog, jumped up and took a long drink from the horse's automatic waterer.

Janie laughed.

"It seems even Pinkerton knows he should hydrate," she giggled.

Mrs. Carter smiled, as Janie finished her drink and placed the riding helmet she'd left hanging on the ring gatepost on her head and fastened the chinstrap.

"I'm ready to ride!" Janie exclaimed.

And then, she handed Mrs. Carter the empty Gatorade bottle and mounted Cheery Day.

Janie opened the gate from atop her mount, just as she had been taught, closed it behind her and entered the ring, stopping far enough behind the first jump to make ready for Mrs. Carter's signal to begin the series of jumps.

Mrs. Carter removed the stopwatch from her pocket, as Janie awaited the nod of Mrs. Carter's head to begin the series of jumps. Pinkerton, the dog, remained at Mrs. Carter's side, as if he had actually understood Janie's previous directive.

And then, it began, all with a nod of Mrs. Carter's head . . . jump after jump, over and over again.

And the times got better and better!

The Howling In Griffin Forest

And then, the lesson was finished; and a breathless, tired Janie, returned to where Mrs. Carter stood, leaning on her cane, Pinkerton, the dog, by her side, tail wagging.

"Better hydrate!" Mrs. Carter said, as she pointed to the bed of her old pickup truck where the cooler filled with Gatorade was waiting. "And better get a Gatorade for me as well," she added. "I got tired just watching you! You really were magnificent today!" she exclaimed.

Janie dismounted Cheery Day and did as she was told. Then she removed Cheery Day's bit and dressed her in a bitless bridle so that she, too, could drink from the automatic waterer.

"I can't wait to see how well you will do in the coming hunter jumper show this weekend," Mrs. Carter told Janie. "I have very, very high expectations for you."

Janie had forgotten all about the upcoming hunter jumper event. But then, she had been somewhat preoccupied with everything else that was happening.

And then, as she sipped her Gatorade, she looked in the direction of Griffin Forest and saw the coyote pack.

"Do you see them?" she asked Mrs. Carter. "Should we be afraid?" she asked, as the coyote pack stood there in the distance.

"I think we'll be quite alright," Mrs. Carter told Janie. "But it does seem like they are getting much bolder," she added, shaking her head.

The Howling In Griffin Forest

And then, after discussing the training session with Janie, and after all of the jumps were placed back in the bed of Mrs. Carter's old, white 2002 Ford F150 pickup truck, the coyote pack turned away and headed back into the forest, much to Janie's great relief. And Janie, atop Cheery Day, rode Cheery Day back to the barn; as Mrs. Carter drove her old, white Ford F150 pickup truck back down to the Griffin Farm farmhouse.

CHAPTER TWENTY-TWO
Once Back At The Farmhouse . . .

Janie methodically went about doing her late afternoon, pre-dinner chores, feeding the animals, greeting Faith, the jersey cow, and putting Cheery day in her stall for the night . . . and then, she walked back to the farmhouse where her mother and Mrs. Carter sat at the kitchen table enjoying glasses of freshly squeezed lemonade.

"I was just telling your mother about the coyotes," Mrs. Carter told Janie, as Janie entered the back kitchen door, letting it slam behind her.

"Please try to not slam the door," her mother said, as she called out to Runty. "Time to eat!" she yelled, as Runty quickly joined them in the kitchen and hopped aboard one of the table chairs.

"Does he often join you at the table?" Mrs. Carter asked Janie's mother.

"Not when we're eating," Janie's mother told Mrs. Carter. "He has his very own eating times."

"I don't know how you do it," Mrs. Carter said. "You do so much! You seem to always be busy doing something," Mrs. Carter added.

"You make time for those you love, all creatures great and small," Janie's mother told her with a rather nonchalant smile.

Janie's mother fetched Runty's special canned dog food from the cupboard, opened the can with the electric can opener, and after she put the dog food into his special dog food bowl that was labeled with his name, she grabbed a spoon from the silverware door, returned to the table, and sat on the chair next to where Runty sat, and she began to spoon feed him.

"This is so much easier than trying to feed him when he's sitting on the floor," Janie's mother said, as spoonful after spoonful of dog food was fed to the now not so small pup.

"Whatever works!" Mrs. Carter told Janie's mother with a smile.

As Janie's mother continued to feed the somewhat oversized pup, Janie's mother's mobile phone rang.

"Will you please get that?" Janie's mother asked Janie, who quickly obliged and went to the kitchen counter to retrieve the phone where her mother had left it.

The Howling In Griffin Forest

"This is Janie!" she said, as she pushed the phone symbol on the phone and put the phone to her ear.

All was momentarily quiet, as Janie's mother continued to feed Runty.

Finally, Janie spoke.

"It's dad!" Janie said. "He says you've been working too hard, and he wants to bring home some pizza and sodas for dinner!" Janie said excitedly.

"How delightful!" Mrs. Carter exclaimed. "I haven't had pizza in ever so long!"

Janie's mother smiled.

"It's a good thing I haven't started dinner," she said.

"Mom says it's a go!" Janie told her father, who promised to be home soon with pizza, bread sticks, an antipasto salad, pepperoncini's, sodas, and strawberry ice-cream for all!

As Janie relayed the message to her mother and Mrs. Carter, her mother sighed. She was somewhat relieved that she didn't have to cook, and for a change could take some time to relax.

When Runty was finished eating, he jumped down from his chair and quietly retired to his bed in the corner of the kitchen, taking a drink first from the bowl of water set next to his bed.

"He really is a special dog," Mrs. Carter said. "And he's so well behaved," she added.

The Howling In Griffin Forest

"He certainly is!" Janie's mother told Mrs. Carter. "And I'm so very glad that we have him."

"So am I!" Janie added.

And then, the three of them sat and talked. And then after a while, Janie got up and got a glass from the kitchen cupboard, sat down, and poured herself a glass of lemonade from the pitcher of lemonade on the kitchen table.

And as they waited, Janie interrupted what she thought was a bland conversation and said, "Tell me some stories about the olden days!"

And Mrs. Carter and her mother laughed.

"Where shall we begin?" Mrs. Carter asked Janie.

"I guess where all stories begin," Janie told her.

"And where is that?" Janie's mother asked.

"Why at the beginning, of course," Janie told them.

And after that, the stories began, as they waited for Janie's father to arrive with the pizza and all of the so-called trimmings and extras. And Janie's mother found this was a more preferred way to pass the time than cooking over a hot stove, at least for today!

CHAPTER TWENTY-THREE
Later That Night

Later that night, Janie lay awake in her bed listening to the howling of the coyotes in the forest. And it seemed to her that the howling was coming closer and closer to the farmhouse. And what made her even *more* concerned was that Pinkerton, the dog, seemed quite concerned himself, as he paced around Janie's bedroom and scratched at Janie's shut door.

"Come here, Pinkerton!" Janie called out to her dog, as she hopped out of her bed and went to where Pinkerton was scratching at her closed bedroom door. "What's the matter, Pinkerton?" she asked, as she kneeled next to the dog to comfort him.

The howling seemed to get closer and louder, and Janie began to wonder if she would get any sleep at all. However, somehow both Janie and Pinkerton, the dog, did manage to finally fall asleep, despite the howling, although it certainly was a restless night.

The Howling In Griffin Forest

The next morning at breakfast, as Janie sat down to a plateful of scrambled eggs with hashbrowns, but no sausage (as she was still on her 'no meat' diet) Janie asked her mother and father, "Did you hear all that howling last night?" And then she added, "I thought it would never stop! And it seemed so close!"

"That's because it *was* close," Janie's father told her.

"It was a bit too close for comfort," Janie's mother added, as Janie's eyes widened.

"Are the horses and other animals safe?" Janie asked.

"I went out early this morning after the howling had stopped, and so far everything is okay. Besides, with the barn doors and all the pens shut, nothing can get in there."

Janie sighed.

"It's kind of scary," she said, under her breath.

"Life is no bowl of cherries," Janie's father told her.

"Speaking of that very thing," Janie's mother interjected, although somewhat off the subject, "I'm going to start a barter system with some of the neighboring farms!"

"Whatever does *that* mean?" Janie's father asked.

"Well, I'm going to trade our extra eggs for milk with the farm across the street until we start getting milk from Faith; and I'm going to can the vegetables and fruit I'll get from the farm down the street in exchange for sharing the jars of what I've canned, with them."

"Really?" Janie's father asked. "You're already doing business with the bee lady down the street.

"Of course, really!" Janie's mother told Janie's father. "It will save everyone time and money if we work together and if we barter our time and our goods with one another, so why not?"

"I just worry you'll be biting off more than you can chew," Janie's father said, as he finished eating and got up from the table to finish readying himself for work.

"I think it's important that we small farmers work together for the good of small farms," Janie's mother told Janie's father, as he walked away from the kitchen table, and as she stood to clear the dishes. "Big agri-business wants to put the small farmer out of business; and we need to do everything we can to save all the small farms, and not be taken over by them."

Hearing that, Janie's father turned in an about face and exclaimed, "You know, you are absolutely right! I never thought of it like that! We do need to work together and help one another!"

And then Janie smiled.

"I'm proud of you!" Janie told her mother. "And if you'll let me, I really do want to help!"

"I'll take you up on that!" Janie's mother said excitedly. "But first, I think you'll need to get ready for that hunter jumper show!"

Janie nodded her head in agreement, and for the moment all of the hullabaloo about the howling coyotes was forgotten. After all, for

The Howling In Griffin Forest

Janie it seemed the entire world lay ahead of her, and she knew she had things to do, and places to go, and people to meet and see! And all of everything that was happening now was very exciting to her, even if the nighttime howling of the coyotes *was* a bit scary.

CHAPTER TWENTY-FOUR
THE WEEK IN REVIEW

Each day for the rest of the week, Janie and her mother and father continued with all of the everyday things that were the usual things they would usually do. Janie's mother set about setting up her bartering and helping Rose, the bee lady, with what was now somewhat of a joint endeavor for the two of them. Janie did all of her usual chores, morning and night, and (of course) dutifully engaged in her training sessions with Mrs. Carter and Cheery Day, with Pinkerton, the dog, watching. And Janie's mother always prepared a virtual feast at dinnertime for all to enjoy; and as the sun went down, the howling in the forest began, much to the dismay of Janie, as well as her mother and father.

Runty was not outgrowing his condition and continued to be spoon fed twice a day by Janie's mother, to which Janie's father asked each day in dismay, "Is it worth it?" And to which Janie's mother would always reassure him that it was indeed worth it, and that she was certain Runty would one day prove to them all that he was most certainly worth her trouble.

The hunter jumper show arrived before anyone knew it, and as Janie performed with Cheery Day in the ring, Janie's father kept saying, "Wow! That is (indeed) poetry in motion!"

Mrs. Carter was quite pleased with Janie and Cheery Day, and everyone was also happily surprised when Janie and Cheery Day were awarded blue ribbons in each event in which Mrs. Carter had entered them.

"I told you she was ready for level six," Mrs. Carter now reminded Janie's mother, as Janie readied Cheery Day for the transport home.

"I'm really tired," Janie told Mrs. Carter, as she carefully guided Cherry day into the horse trailer.

"I'm so proud of you, Kidlet!" her father told her, and Janie's mother agreed.

"You were great out there," she told Janie, as Janie remained silent.

"I think she's had enough excitement for one day," Mrs. Carter told Janie's mother and father, to which they wholeheartedly nodded their heads in agreement.

Finally, Janie's father spoke.

The Howling In Griffin Forest

"How about if we all go out for a celebratory dinner?" he asked.

"But I don't eat meat!" Janie protested, somewhat in vain, as she waited for her father's response.

"And so, you will have a nice vegetarian burger," her father told her. "And you can even have a salad and a dessert!" he added emphatically.

And that made Janie smile.

"And I know just the place!" Janie's mother interjected. "Why don't we go to the Hard Rock Café?"

"I love that place!" Mrs. Carter exclaimed.

"And so do I!" Janie told her mother, as she looked at her father, wide-eyed.

"Then, we're off to eat!" Janie's father exclaimed.

And then there was a pause.

"But what about Cheery Day?" Janie asked her father. "She can't exactly go to a restaurant, and I don't like the idea of leaving her standing in the horse trailer when she must be even more tired than I am!"

"Then, we'll all go back to the farmhouse and put her in the barn; and then we'll go to eat!"

"I'll follow you," Mrs. Carter said. "Hard Rock Café isn't too far from the farmhouse. Then we can all go together!"

And so, it was decided.

The Howling In Griffin Forest

"That's a plan!" Janie's father said.

"And we may as well feed all the animals while we're there," Janie added.

"And I will gladly and happily help you with that!" Mrs. Carter said, as she leaned on her cane.

And so it was, and they all headed for Griffin Farm.

CHAPTER TWENTY-FIVE
Gone Like The Wind

When they arrived at Griffin Farm, Mrs. Carter in her truck, and Janie and her mom and dad in their truck, pulling Cheery Day in the horse trailer behind them, everything seemed normal, except for one thing. The sky above them was becoming quite dark and foreboding.

"It shouldn't be getting dark this early," Janie's mother surmised, as she exited the truck and looked up at the grey of the darkening sky.

Mrs. Carter got out of her truck and leaned on her cane.

"I think we might be in the eye of a storm," Mrs. Carter told Janie's mother. "I suggest we get the horses all into the barn."

"Oh, I took care of that before we left this morning," Janie told Mrs. Carter, as they headed for the house. "I never put them out to pasture today."

The Howling In Griffin Forest

Janie's mother gave Janie a skewed look.

"You didn't put them out at all?" Janie's mother asked Janie somewhat concerned that Janie hadn't fully performed her daily chores.

"Well, I think that just may have been a good idea," Mrs. Carter said, as the wind began to blow.

And then, it happened. The coyote pack began to howl. They moved quickly from the far side of the farmhouse to a point where Janie, her mother and her father and Mrs. Carter could see them. There eyes seemed to glow, and the head of the pack began to growl.

"We'd better get inside," Mrs. Carter said, as she hobbled on her cane toward the front door of the old farmhouse.

One by one they all entered the farmhouse, as the coyotes grew braver and braver, and came closer and closer to where they were.

"But what about Cheery Day?" Janie asked, as she went through the door. "I haven't gotten her out of the horse trailer yet. And I still have to feed the animals as well! What about them?"

"Don't you fret," Mrs. Carter said, reassuringly. "Cheery Day and the rest of the animals will be just fine."

And then, as Janie entered the farmhouse, with her mother following closely behind her, Runty suddenly appeared from the other side of the farmhouse, barking and growling, all alone and all by himself!

The Howling In Griffin Forest

Janie's mother screamed as she jutted through the door, letting it slam behind her.

Janie's father was still outside.

"What about dad?" Janie screamed, as her father ran back to the family truck and jumped inside the cab's front seat.

"He ran back to the truck, and he's safe there," Janie's mother told Janie, trying to remain composed.

Runty kept running in the direction of the coyotes.

"Runty! Runty!" Janie screamed, fearful for the dog's safety.

And then, it happened. The lead coyote let out a very large yelp, and the coyote pack fled back into the forest with our not so little Runty (who was now eighty-five pounds) chasing them all the way!

And then, as suddenly as it had started, the wind stopped, and the skies opened. And the coyotes were gone with the wind!

Runty returned to the farmhouse, receiving words of praise; and Janie's mother turned and looked at Janie's father as if to say, 'I told you so', and all was right with the world.

"I think Runty showed them who's boss!" Mrs. Carter exclaimed. "And I do think your coyote troubles are over and done with now!"

Janie's mother beamed. Runty had shown his worth, and all was well with their world now. Janie's mother spoon fed Runty, with not a word of complaint or question from Janie's father. And Janie took Cheery Day out of the horse trailer, put Cheery Day in her stall, and fed all the animals, as everyone else freshened up; and then they all went out for that celebratory dinner.

They all had vegie burgers, onion rings, salads, sodas, and all you can eat fries, with cherry cheesecake for dessert. And (of course) the adults all had their after-dinner coffee.

And later that night, the coyotes didn't howl; and for the first time in a long time, and for days thereafter, everyone slept in quiet slumber. And it was all thanks to Runty, the puppy Janie's mother dutifully spoon fed twice a day!

And Janie's mother could not help but to smile at Runty, every single time, every single day thereafter, as she looked down at her now not so little pup!

"Sometimes, some packages hold big surprises!" she told Runty later that fateful night, after they returned home from their celebratory dinner.

And Janie and her father both wholeheartedly agreed, because Runty had most certainly saved the day, that day! And he was (indeed) a true doggy hero! And besides that, he was quite lovable to boot! And what had happened just went to prove that every day at Griffin Farm brought even more fun and adventure, even though there was always work to be done, and even though sometimes it seemed like the work was never finished. But that was okay! Because, you see, it was all worth it!

www.ingramcontent.com/pod-product-compliance
Lightning Source LLC
LaVergne TN
LVHW021943060526
838200LV00042B/1914